SHOPPING
WORDS

Jenny Tyler
Illustrated by Sue Stitt

With consultant advice from John Newson and Gillian Hartley
of the Child Development Research Unit at Nottingham
University, and Robyn Gee.

abc

shop

counter

bag

packet

scales

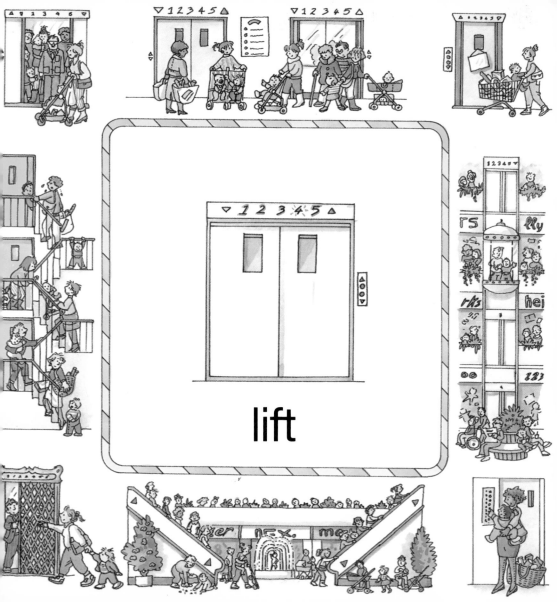

lift

mirror

purse

trolley

drink

counter

trolley

lift

packet

mirror

bag

drink

shop

purse

scales